HELPING YOUR BRAND-NEW READER

Here's how to make first-time reading easy and fun:

▌ Read the introduction at the beginning of each story aloud. Look through the pictures together so that your child can see what happens in the story before reading the words.

▌ Read the first page to your child, placing your finger under each word.

▌ Let your child touch the words and read the rest of the story. Give him or her time to figure out each new word.

▌ If your child gets stuck on a word, you might say, *"Try something. Look at the picture. What would make sense?"*

▌ If your child is still stuck, supply the right word. This will allow him or her to continue to read and enjoy the story. You might say, *"Could this word be 'ball'?"*

▌ Always praise your child. Praise what he or she reads correctly, and praise good tries too.

▌ Give your child lots of chances to read the story again and again. The more your child reads, the more confident he or she will become.

▌ Have fun!

First edition 2001

Library of Congress Cataloging-in-Publication Data

Samton, Sheila White.
Hurray for Rosa! / Sheila White Samton. — 1st ed.
p.   cm. — (Brand new readers)
Summary: Four brief adventures of Rosa as she imitates animals,
goes to the beach, makes a sandwich, and has a birthday cake.
ISBN 0-7636-1126-3
[1. Food — Fiction. 2. Beaches — Fiction.
3. Animals — Fiction.] I. Title. II. Series.
PZ7.S185 Mo 2001
[E] — dc21   00-049369

2 4 6 8 10 9 7 5 3 1

Printed in Hong Kong

This book was typeset in Letraset Arta.
The illustrations were done in gouache.

Candlewick Press
2067 Massachusetts Avenue
Cambridge, Massachusetts 02140

visit us at www.candlewick.com

HURRAY FOR ROSA!

CANDLEWICK PRESS
CAMBRIDGE, MASSACHUSETTS

WRITTEN AND ILLUSTRATED BY **Sheila White Samton**

Contents

ROSA AT THE FARM

Introduction

This story is called *Rosa at the Farm*.
It is about what each animal does and
then what Rosa does.

A duck quacks.

Rosa quacks.

5

A cow moos.

Rosa moos.

A worm crawls.

8

Rosa crawls.

A bird flies.

Rosa falls!

ROSA AT THE BEACH

Introduction

This story is called *Rosa at the Beach*.
It is about what Rosa puts on before going
in the water, and then what she does after
she goes in the water.

Rosa is at the beach.

Rosa puts on her swim cap.

Rosa puts on her mask.

Rosa puts on her flippers.

17

Rosa puts on her life preserver.

18

SPLASH!

Rosa is cold.

Rosa reads her book.

ROSA'S SANDWICH

21

Introduction

This story is called *Rosa's Sandwich*.
It is about all the things Rosa gets to
make a sandwich.

Rosa gets bread.

24

Rosa gets peanut butter.

Rosa gets ketchup.

Rosa gets a pickle.

Rosa gets marshmallows.

Rosa gets a banana.

Rosa makes a sandwich.

Rosa gives the sandwich to Pablo.

HAPPY BIRTHDAY, ROSA!

31

Introduction

This story is called *Happy Birthday, Rosa!*
It is about how Rosa cuts her cake and
gives a piece to each person in her family.

"Happy birthday, Rosa!"

Rosa cuts her cake.

"Here is Grandma's piece."

"Here is Grandpa's piece."

37

"Here is Papa's piece."

"Here is Mama's piece."

"Here is Pablo's piece."

40

"Here is Rosa's piece."